PSYCHOLOGY
OF THE
Rich Aunt

D1713222

ERICH MÜHSAM

PSYCHOLOGY
OF THE
Rich Aunt

Being an Inquiry

in Twenty-Five Parts

into the Question of Immortality

TRANSLATED BY ERIK BUTLER

WAKEFIELD PRESS

CAMBRIDGE, MASSACHUSETTS

Originally published as *Die Psychologie der Erbtante: Eine Tanthologie aus 25 Einzeldarstellungen als Beitrag zur Lösung der Unsterblichkeits-Frage* (Zurich: Verlag Caesar Schmidt, 1905).

This book was set in Garamond Premier Pro and Helvetica Neue Pro by Wakefield Press. Printed and bound by McNaughton & Gunn, Inc., in the United States of America.

ISBN: 978-1-939663-37-5

Available through D.A.P./Distributed Art Publishers
75 Broad Street, Suite 630
New York, New York 10004
Tel: (212) 627-1999
Fax: (212) 627-9484

10   9   8   7   6   5   4   3   2   1

CONTENTS

EUROPEAN CIVIL WAR AND THE OCCULT AUNT

> Constant revolutionizing of production, uninterrupted disturbance of all social conditions, everlasting uncertainty and agitation distinguish the bourgeois epoch from all earlier ones. All fixed, fast-frozen relations, with their train of ancient and venerable prejudices and opinions, are swept away. . . . All that is solid melts into air, all that is holy is profaned, and man is at last compelled to face with sober senses his real conditions of life, and his relations with his kind.
>
> Karl Marx, *The Communist Manifesto*

Erich Mühsam (1878–1934) was born in Berlin to Jewish parents and grew to be a freethinker and anarchist with communist leanings.[1] His first decades included being expelled from school for political agitation at the age of sixteen, joining an artists' commune, performing in cabarets, and generally cultivating what qualifies as an alternative lifestyle. All of this occurred during a tumultuous period of German—and world—history. At the end of the "Great War," Mühsam also played a key role in the short-lived Bavarian Soviet Republic inspired by the Bolshevik coup in Russia.

None of this was suited to endear Mühsam to the likes of Adolf Hitler, who also spent years in a bohemian milieu but veered in the opposite political direction.[2] (Both men went to prison for seditious activity in the Weimar Republic and were amnestied by the same decree.) The Nazis rose to power promising to clean up polluted race and culture—"degeneration" in Max Nordau's ominous, nineteenth-century phrasing. Shortly after Hitler's regime had started making Germany great again, Mühsam met a horrible end at the Oranienburg concentration camp. He was found hanging in the latrines, battered beyond recognition.

The native element of radicalism is conflict. It grabs reality at the root (*radix*) and can wrench it left, right, or both ways at once. To account for misadventures in Western Christendom during the first half of the twentieth century, some historians speak of the "Second Thirty Years War" from 1914 to 1945. Alternatively, "European Civil War" refers to the same period, which was defined by imperial intrigue, economic crises, ethnic chauvinism, and militant utopianism.[3] Of course, historical periodization is inexact. Like mental and physical illness, tensions fester, erupt, and go into remission; they can destroy from within, even when the overall balance of health seems relatively stable. Communism was not the only specter haunting Europe. The Führer was not the only false messiah. Mühsam was certainly not the only victim.

Our hero stood and fell with the vanquished. In 1911, Mühsam founded *Kain* (Cain), a journal named in honor of the farmer whose offerings a tyrannical deity spurned in favor of blood sacrifice. His earlier vegetarian anthem ("Gesang der Vegetarier") had declared that the world would be a better place without "corpse-eaters" and their primitive faith. Mühsam always affirmed the right to modern-day noble savagery: freedom from religious mystification, overbearing state and family structures, and alienating relations of production. Another poem, "Christmas" ("Weihnachten"), concludes with a beggar picking the story of Jesus's birth out of the gutter and wiping his ass with it. In jail for his convictions and activities, Mühsam wrote *Judas: A Workers' Drama in Five Acts* (1920). He never compromised or capitulated.

Psychology of the Rich Aunt (1905) exemplifies the heretical verve animating the author's life and work. This short book presents twenty-five portraits of women who leave the deserving and undeserving generations that succeed them empty-handed. While entertaining, the vignettes also form a short circuit that throws sparks. On the one hand, Mühsam promises "psychology." On the other hand, he declares that he is demonstrating the immortality of the soul. The former term refers to studying the mind in analogy to the physical organism, as an embodied system. Proof of immortality, in contrast, is a theological endeavor and bears on the eternal spirit. Psychology has a corporeal orbit; theology looks to the stars and beyond.

The space between reified science and gaseous metaphysics ignites on the flint of materialism: unsublimated want. Mühsam makes himself the spokesman of the disinherited, who are as fit as anyone to enjoy the earth's bounty. It's a positive fact that aunts won't die when their nieces and nephews wish; their true legacy is always a surprise. Ergo, aunts harbor hidden ("occult") power: the capacity to reverse fortune. Like the mysterious "commodity fetish" described in *Capital*, these agents of tribal alliance exercise a negative influence on the flow of resources, which would occur freely in a state of nature.

Conspirators know the importance of artful silence, reading between the lines, and—when the time is right—decisive action.

If "fixed, fast-frozen relations, with their train of ancient and venerable prejudices and opinions" are already in the course of being "swept away," some might need a little push.

Mühsam wrote satire, and satire works by code. Accordingly, *Psychology of the Rich Aunt* offers a wealth of zany situations and types (to say nothing of nods to other troublemakers awaiting rediscovery).[4] The radical's task is not to describe the world, but to change it. Under the mask of humor, the author wounds "ancient and venerable prejudices and opinions." Mühsam might clown around, but he's not shooting blanks. "Cutting" and "trenchant" aspects of his style aren't metaphors, either. "All that is holy is profaned," starting with the holiest of all: kinship and property.

Since the prevailing conditions of Mühsam's day have hardly given way to a fairer and better world, the existential slapstick is still timely—and funny, too. But by the same token, it's depressing. In sending up what he calls "prevailing falsehoods," Mühsam's alter ego is consistently hoisted by his own petard. The irony may or may not have escaped the author. If it didn't, he qualifies as a tragic figure. Over and over, blind self-interest proves as burdensome as an ancestral curse, congenital deformity, or revolution betrayed.

The oblivion into which Mühsam has fallen is cruel, but not a shock. As his slightly younger but more celebrated contemporary Walter Benjamin observed, having "character" means defying "fate"; and fate—the circumstances and conditions in which human action necessarily occurs—looks like guilt, even if it isn't.[5] Exhibiting character belongs to the sphere of freedom, but *being* a character marks the limits of individual potential: "with sober senses," one "is compelled to face" mortality.

Mühsam had too much character to escape the force of destiny, whether it's written in the stars or results from human perversity. Nor does inborn dignity equal innocence. In the end, man must confront "his real conditions . . . and his relations with his kind." Real conditions and relations with one's kind, during a civil war, stink like communal toilets—or an open grave.

Erik Butler

NOTES

1. For biographical information and key documents, see Erich Mühsam, *Liberating Society from the State and Other Writings: A Political Reader*, trans. Gabriel Kuhn (Oakland: PM Press, 2011).

2. See Albrecht Koschorke, *On Hitler's Mein Kampf: The Poetics of National Socialism*, trans. Erik Butler (Cambridge, MA: MIT Press, 2017).

3. For a succinct and compelling account, see Enzo Traverso, *Fire and Blood: The European Civil War 1914–1945*, trans. David Fernbach (London: Verso, 2016).

4. E.g., "Dolorosa" (Maria Eichhorn, b. 1879)—one of Mühsam's real-life associates—who composed and performed sadomasochistic verse before vanishing from the European scene without a trace.

5. Discussing the poetry of Friedrich Hölderlin, Benjamin observes that only "the blissful gods" have ever been called "fateless"—and they never dared to live in the first place. (Walter Benjamin, "Fate and Character," *Selected Writings*, vol. 1, *1913–1926*, ed. Marcus Bullock and Michael W. Jennings [Cambridge, MA: Harvard University Press, 2002], 201–206, 203.)

PSYCHOLOGY
OF THE
Rich Aunt

INTRODUCTION

———

This book has not been written to swell the burgeoning ranks of literature with another raw recruit. Rather, it responds to the urgent need to fortify, with one more brick, the edifice upon which philosophers and theologians, poets and thinkers, have labored since time immemorial. An answer to the question of immortality, human and otherwise, would represent the attainment of perfect knowledge. The matter holds such importance for the social, psychic, and physical life of individuals and peoples—regarding, as it does, whether they are *to be or not to be*—that I have made bold to share my own, partial views. If nothing else, I hope the same will further the interests of truth.

None other than Gotthold Ephraim Lessing made a contribution to the proof of immortality when, in a profound, epigrammatic meditation, he praised an educational establishment for girls:

> Think, how wholesome and pure the air
> Must be around that school there;
> In its halls, since the dawn of time,
> Was never a young *lady* left behind.

However, where the poet only credits the inmates of one institution with the excellent quality of immortality, I will go a giant step further and, in the book at hand, offer proof that a whole genus of human beings exists which is immune to the Grim Reaper's scythe: *Rich Aunts*.

The problem is too weighty, its discussion too great in import, for me to waste time on long-winded polemics—explaining my findings to skeptical pedants who shut their ears against all that is new or that otherwise unsettles prejudice. In a word and stated summarily: The Rich Aunt is immortal! Twenty-five examples follow, that the world may decide whether my observations are meritorious, and conclusions justified.

The form that—and the standard under which—this epoch-making discovery should be made public provided the object of considerable debate and reflection. Much gnashing of teeth and racking of brains attended the title, in particular.

Psychology or physiology? That was the question. Initially, I inclined toward the latter. After all, is not dying—and, all the more, not-dying—not a physiological process? And yet, does not-dying not constitute a character trait much more than a mental defect, especially in the case of the Rich Aunt? This consideration ultimately carried the day. The twenty-five exemplars mustered below will validate my decision to call the book *Psychology of the Rich Aunt*.

A further difficulty arose as regards the ladies' order of appearance. To be sure, it would have been only right that my aunts parade according to seniority. That said, it proved impossible to determine their respective age in most cases. What is more, I deemed it unseemly and lacking due respect to stir up ancient and long-buried points of petty jealousy by disclosing one aunt's lack of youth relative to another. Alphabetic sequence alone would protect me from universal hostility and enable objective assessment of the facts.

A need deeply felt besets our age, which this book would address: finally to shed light on the mystery of the Rich Aunt's earthly ways. I would fain remove the scales from the eyes of all who anticipate the bounteous bequest of one aunt or another—only to experience, time and again, the shock of hopes deceived. I would prove, once and for all, the folly and rashness of that youth, who advertised in the local paper that he would gladly exchange three ordinary aunts for a single rich one.

Indeed, it is my hope to help ordinary aunts obtain their due by acknowledging that their rights, as members of human society, equal those of Rich Aunts—that is, equal the rights of ladies whose title of nobility brands them the very incarnation of prevailing falsehoods.

Erich Mühsam

AUNT AMALIA

———

At the bottom of her heart, she was a good woman, and she had a lot—some say a whole lot—of money. Plus, she was at least twenty-five years older than she told anyone who asked. Is it any wonder that three nephews—Hans, Ferdinand, and Eberhard—and four nieces—Charlotte, Anni, Else, and Paula—idolized Aunt Amalia?

Aunt Amalia acquired her fortune after many years of widowhood. Her husband, Uncle Theodor, had been a goodly furrier. Cleaning furs and storing them for commensurate payment in summertime and supplying elegant society with warm, new muffs in winter, he had, for better or worse, provided for himself and Aunt Amalia (who, appropriate efforts notwithstanding, remained without issue). His last Christmas on earth, he gave his better half a ticket in the horse market lottery. It was drawn the very first round. Having festively transferred the proceeds from the carriage and team of four to his spouse—three thousand marks—he passed away. Aunt Amalia subtracted the funds necessary for his interment and the purchase of a quarter ticket in the Saxony State

Lottery. She put the rest in an interest-bearing account at the bank administrated by Truggold & Co. (reg. LLC).

Her number was drawn once more, and Aunt Amalia bought herself another ticket: this time, a whole half-ticket in the Thuringia Lottery. Fortune smiled again—and then again and again. Eventually, she had won the state lottery in twenty-six German fatherlands. Her unheard-of luck soon enabled her to retire and live on the interest her assets earned, paid in monthly installments by Truggold & Co. (reg. LLC). Thereby, she advanced from the modest estate of regular aunt to the condition of Rich Aunt for her three nephews and four nieces.

Meanwhile, these seven heirs had formed a mutual insurance company by contracting engagements with each other. Hans got engaged to Paula, Ferdinand to Anni, and Eberhard to Else. The eldest niece, Charlotte, remained unengaged. The charter foresaw that she alone would be the beneficiary of her share—so she might, in turn, be a lucky Rich Aunt for her own nephews and nieces.

One evening, the seven heirs were gathered in a shareholders' meeting. Charlotte was reading to the others from the paper—"local news"—and suddenly cried out. Something terrible had happened: the intendant of the banking house Truggold & Co. (reg. LLC), Moses Truggold, had abandoned ship with six million marks—and in the company of a young lady from the circus. The "firm" was insolvent.

The seven heirs rushed in horror to Aunt Amalia, that she might still save what was left to be saved. They came too late.

Aunt Amalia was a Rich Aunt no more. She was slumping forward in her chair, the newspaper opened to the sad tidings of the collapse of Truggold & Co. (reg. LLC).

The nephews and nieces besieged her with questions but received no answer. Aunt Amalia was dead, felled by a stroke.

The mutual insurance association disbanded. Charlotte abandoned hope that a bequest would make her a Rich Aunt, too. Like the dear departed, once upon a time, she commended her fate to the lotto.

AUNT BERTHA

———

Every afternoon at three o'clock, Aunt Bertha took the green watering can off the nail, donned her red Turkish shawl, and went to the churchyard opposite which, for the last twenty-three years, she had lived for convenience's sake. Then she headed down the fifth row and seated herself on the bench next to the sixteenth grave, where her spouse, a retired tax collector, had laid at rest for the last twenty-four years.

Once Aunt Bertha had wiped a teardrop from the yellow wrinkle running from the pit once denominated "eye" down to the corner of her mouth, she drew from the right-hand pocket of her grayish black pinafore an unfinished stocking, and from the left-hand pocket a paper cornet of chocolate drops. Under rainy conditions, she would open a violet-dotted umbrella she had left here for this express purpose. Then she started to knit, suck, and think.

Verily, Aunt Bertha thought. She thought much and profoundly, and did not stop until her eyes grew heavy.

At precisely six o'clock, the venerable sexton would come and wake her.

What Aunt Bertha thought about so much and so profoundly was weighty indeed. In the course of her years of widowhood, she had saved nearly 30,000 marks; she had still not made a will, even though she knew what she wanted to happen with the money. Twenty thousand would go to her only near relation, Nephew Emil—who, were she to die intestate, would receive the whole inheritance. She intended that the difference be used to set up the Biefke Foundation, which would pay taxes that the clientele of tax collector Biefke, of blessed memory, still had to make yearly.

True, few of those her husband had relieved of extra pecuniary weight remained among the living. But one party in particular had such a great income that every year he shoveled more into the public purse than the 350 marks she earned in interest would cover. Once said party had died, her capital would prove sufficient. Aunt Bertha duly decided not to draw up a will before the factory owner Lehmeyer had closed his eyes forever.

Yet Herr Lehmeyer was but sixty-five, and hale and hearty, whereas Aunt Bertha had reached the age of seventy-nine and wobbled ominously at the jaw. Those who knew that she was waiting for Herr Lehmeyer's demise deemed her a thing of wonder. For his part, nephew Emil wrote in his journal: "As a clerk in the employ of Eduard

Bindemann, my income is 3,000 marks per year. I need this money for living expenses. If Aunt Bertha does as she intends and leaves me 20,000 marks, this sum will yield an additional 700 marks interest. That would permit me to live a little better. But if she dies without a will, the boss will make me his partner, and I'll get half of the company revenue. Then I'll be able to get married."

Thus did Emil reckon. And since he was eager to marry, he had every incentive to ensure that Aunt Bertha not somehow write a will, after all. He knew her habits, however, and on this basis contrived an iniquitous scheme, which he put into action on a rainy autumn day. In the early morning, he stole to Uncle Biefke's graveside, seized Aunt Bertha's violet-dotted umbrella—which now, as ever, was leaning on the bench—and slinked off with his plunder.

Fine but steady rainfall began at noon. When Aunt Bertha arrived at the wonted hour, she wiped the obligatory teardrop from the yellow wrinkle, drew the unfinished stocking from the right pocket of her dress and the chocolate drops from the left, and then made ready to open her umbrella. Realizing it was not there, she collapsed in fright. After she had been brought to the safety of her home, she lay abed, pastor and prayer book to her left, legal notary and documents to her right; straightaway, she had sent for them, thinking of nothing but her last will and testament.

Mortal terror at the purloined umbrella had deprived her of much sense. When the lawyer asked who should come into the inheritance, the only thought that occurred to her was that Emil should not get it all, and she gasped: "Not Emil!" That was all she managed. Accordingly, the notary wrote that Aunt Bertha was disinheriting her nephew; he could not find out who should take the latter's place, and her forces were fading fast, so he hastened to obtain her signature—which, with the pastor's aid, he was just able to obtain.

She died. Since her sole relative had been exheridated, Father State intervened and raked in the 30,000 marks with a complaisant grin. Wayward Emil was left standing—but with an umbrella.

AUNT CHRISTINE

———

This time, it had to be true. My friend Ernst Frohgesinnt had rushed to me in tears to tell me about it. And I was happy to believe him. He was such a nice fellow that he had a break coming—and Aunt Christine was such a dear old spinster that if anybody could be trusted to dispel my skepticism about Rich Aunts, it was her.

There was no longer any room for doubt. Aunt Christine had named Ernst Frohgesinnt, her only nephew and nearest relation, the sole heir of her entire fortune of 45,000 marks. Indeed, she was so kind that she had looked on, very much alive, as he joyfully read her will.

Ernst was rapturous. That evening, we went to the Kaiserkeller and hoisted one glass of wine after the next to Aunt Christine's health and painless promotion to glory.

Ernst built golden palaces in the air. First, he would get married to his little Liesl; their engagement had lasted three years already. He would have his poems printed, then they would take a trip south so his sickly lungs could grow strong again. His face beamed with cheer. And as the red spots on his cheeks spread across his face, it even seemed the wine had painted good health on it! . . . The next day, I paid a visit to Aunt Christine. As her nephew's friend, I deemed it wise to be seen now and then. Since learning about her magnanimous testament, I felt an especially strong urge to do so.

I really was fond of the old lady. Of all the aunts I have ever met, she truly was one of the most sympathetic. Her face was round and friendly, with clever, kindly eyes that would light up whenever conversation turned to her nephew Ernst Frohgesinnt. I called her "auntie," too— this diminutive, lively person you couldn't help but like, once you'd gotten to know her.

She was always dressed in a black, silk dress fringed with costly lace; on top, she wore an elegant black pinafore with a ring of jingling keys protruding from the left-hand pocket. A spick-and-span bonnet crowned her gray hair, and dangling gold earrings rounded out the picture. She looked like one of those dear aunties in nineteenth-century novels, who use a little ruse to help young girls finally get the man of their dreams, even though a hundred obstacles stand in the way. After a spirited and heartfelt greeting, she offered me a glass of wine and a cigar—she was always ready for visitors—and then chattered away lightheartedly.

She spoke of her childhood and engagement; she had been set to marry a strapping young coxswain—how often had I heard the tale!—but he drowned in a ship-wreck three weeks before the day of their nuptials. Ever since, she had dressed in mourning and dedicated her life to his memory.

Now, of course, she had overcome the deep sorrow that had made her shun the world for decades. She regaled me with cheerful and vivid little episodes from happier days. I could hear them again and again: everything she said matched her demeanor and character so perfectly, it never grew old.

Then she would come to speak of Ernst. Yes, there was something about his personality and bearing just like her beau. It's just such a shame that his health isn't better! Well, when she was dead, he wouldn't need to worry about scrabbling around for something to eat; he'd be able to take care of himself just fine. It didn't occur to her that she might help him now, but she positively glowed with pride at the thought of one day lifting the poor boy out of crushing poverty. She had had her will notarized—now she could die in peace.

But that's not how it happened.

Ernst Frohgesinnt experienced a massive pulmonary hemorrhage. A week later, he was dead. Aunt Christine didn't survive him for long. Grief at the loss of her dear nephew struck her down just after she had changed her will to divide her estate between a society for the prevention of cruelty to animals and a theater cooperative. Aunt Christine had always been crazy about the theater.

AUNT DOROTHEA

———

She was dying.

At last!

Eighty-seven years is a long time for the earthly so-journ of a lady who has preserved her maiden state. And Aunt Dorothea was eighty-seven years old.

Now she was dying.

Who could be more delighted than her only neph-ew and heir, Konrad?

Konrad bought a bouquet of carnations and headed for Aunt Dorothea's deathbed. When he arrived, she was still wheezing. With the narrow whites of her eyes (which was all that could now be seen of them, apart from a little red above and below), she cast a loving gaze.

The dutiful nephew took a pin—he always held pins at the ready, under the collar of his vest—and fastened the carnations to Aunt Dorothea's blouse. Neither he nor she even noticed that he also stuck the pin through the yellow-brown parchment of her skin wilting below in loose folds.

Aunt Dorothea wanted to smell flowers again, even though she was quite asthmatic. So she poked her nose, which already extended pretty far over the covers, and sniffed at the carnations. Then her head sank back down. Her time was up.

Konrad pressed her eyes closed and went home. Evening fell; he went to bed and slept soundly.—

When Aunt Dorothea had been buried, the courts notified Konrad that Aunt Dorothea had named him her sole heir. At his earliest convenience, he should kindly inform them whether he was willing to enter into the inheritance.

"Dear old aunt!" Nephew Konrad grinned. Then he pulled out a sheet of scratch paper and graciously apprised the court that he would, in fact, agree to receive Aunt Dorothea's bequest at his earliest convenience. Evening fell; he went to bed and slept soundly.——

It was all quite opportune for poor Konrad. He faced appalling circumstances. On all sides, he was badgered and besieged. Now, help had arrived: Aunt Dorothea's fortune was not slight. Nephew Konrad would daydream about getting his hands on the money. Every evening, he went to bed in cheerful anticipation of his dream becoming reality—and slept more soundly than ever.

Three weeks passed in this way. Then Konrad got a letter bearing a seal, official business requiring postage. Trembling in joyous expectation, he surrendered the requisite twenty pfennigs. He was quite sure it was an invitation to come and retrieve Aunt Dorothea's bequest—finally, his beggary would be over and done.

Poor Konrad! The missive indicated that Aunt Dorothea had indeed left a fortune of 80,000 marks. However, for the past fifty years, she had dodged three-quarters of the taxes she owed, which would be subtracted from the money. What is more, the heirs—or, in this case, heir—"are hereby notified that a penalty of 1200 marks *pro anno*" was being levied. In sum: 60,000 + 6% of fifty years' worth of 60,000 marks in unpaid taxes, mercifully omitting compound interest (which the revenue officer probably didn't know the math for):

Penalty	60,000 marks
+ payment in arrears (3600 x 50)	180,000 marks
	240,000 marks

In a word: "Two hundred forty thousand marks, payment due within eight days."

Konrad collapsed. "It's a wash," he sobbed.

That night he did not sleep soundly. He slept with the fishes.

AUNT ELFRIEDE

The psychology of this Rich Aunt, Aunt Elfriede, proved quite difficult for me. She was an earth mother in body and soul, a veritable Valkyrie, with arms as mighty as the boughs of a centenarian German oak, and hands as vast as serving dishes. Before her I felt a pagan's fear.

Aunt Elfriede was crafty, to boot. Unspeakably so. I can still see her before me, brandishing her great appendages and uttering her innermost heart's desires in a booming voice that sounded like a Wagner tuba with buttered bread stuck in its craw. These stirrings of her heart bore on the whole of Aunt Elfriede's fortune. O woe is me!

Aunt Elfriede fell ill, very ill, mortally ill. The doctor came and went three times a day. I never left her bedside. This was quite perilous, for Aunt Elfriede had visions and raved. She waved her fists in the air and cursed me to no end for just waiting for her to die; I learned that she had beaten her husband until his final day, then trampled him with those legs—legs I saw under the covers several times, kicking up things—such things, my God!!

Once, when there was a lull in the storm, I thought it heralded the beginning of the end. I took the doctor aside. "Herr Doktor," said I, "Tell me the truth! Is Aunt Elfriede going to die?" He looked at me sadly, cleared his throat, and replied: "My dear, young friend!" I took an audible breath. "Prepare for the worst!" His hand gripped mine. "Your Lady Aunt"—he swallowed several times and made a deep sigh—"Your Lady Aunt is on the way . . ."—"to the hereafter!" my inner voice chimed in—". . . on the way to getting better." He fell silent. "Thank you," I said aloud—then, to myself, "you bastard!" I promptly regained Aunt Elfriede's bedchamber.

She was squinting at me furtively and must have read the disappointment on my face. Suddenly, she sprang up—redoubtably towering atop the pillow. My God, it scares me now just to think how she looked. Her legs were hirsute and the nightshirt appallingly short. She clenched her fists. Her mighty bosom heaved.

"Despicable wretch!" she howled. "I see right through you! Just wait, I won't do you the favor. Eight days from now, I'll be up and about. But you'll taste my awful revenge, you hypocrite, you impostor! You—you—you——You're disinherited!" she gasped. Then she sank back down, utterly spent.

"You're disinherited!" The terrible pronouncement followed me everywhere for the next eight days. And lo, Aunt Elfriede was up and about.

"You're disinherited—you're disinherited!" She really did it.

The next day, she had a relapse. A week later, she died.

For shame, Aunt Elfriede, for shame!

AUNT FRIEDERIKE

———

I wasn't going to inherit much from Aunt Friederike. All the same, it would be the whole widow's allowance constituting her modest but adequate keep. If nothing else, it would permit a pleasant trip to Switzerland or a few months of the high life.

The inheritance was a sure thing—a done deal. I was her only near relation and the sole person who looked after her in her widow's solitude—the only one who came every Sunday, rain or shine, to sit in her cozy little parlor as her newest wingèd words took flight. For Aunt Friederike was a poetess. What aunt—especially if she's got some money—doesn't have a weakness or two? Given her sickly constitution, her end couldn't be long in coming. Dutifully, I let her lyrical effusions rain down on me every week.

The first outpourings to which I was privy—shortly after the death of her husband, who is said to have beaten her frequently before getting his comeuppance after spending an evening too deep in his cups—almost all concerned the suffering of a young widow. Evidently, she felt the pain especially at night.

To facilitate a picture of Aunt Friederike on the basis of her art, allow me to include a sampling from that period:

Wandering through the house by day,
My gaze seeks and does not find you.
Though most often you were away,
Now it is terrible what I go through.
Then at night, when I go to rest,
To lie in bed, sad and lonely,
Tears in my eyes, and woe in my breast:
O dear Heinrich, my one and only!

I had to be honest and tell her what I really thought of her poems. Naturally, a deep sense of duty compelled me to declare them beautiful and profound.

Once, I suggested that she try her hand at what our modern bluestockings pursue so avidly: erotic verse. "You know, that's what the public wants nowadays," I told her, "It can't be too hard for a young woman like you, Aunt Friederike." The next time I came to visit, she declaimed the following:

How my heart is torn asunder
Deep in the dead of night.
In vain, I seek and wonder,
What still might set things right?
Poor widow, I pine and languish
For you and your sweet embrace.

Could I but assuage my anguish,
With something to take your place.

When she finished, she was exhausted. I'm quite sure she meant every word. Alas, this kind of poetry took too much out of her, and soon she died. When the will was read, I learned that she had indeed declared me her sole heir. It would be quite wrong, however, to conclude that the doctrine of the book at hand is thereby disproven.

For Aunt Friederike had stipulated one condition: that posterity might yet learn something of her artistry, her literary remains—filling three dressers and a wardrobe—were to be published. I acted in accordance with her will—which meant using up the whole inheritance and adding another 123 marks and 75 pfennigs from my own pocket. Ever since, I have shunned lady poets.

AUNT GERTA

I have christened you Gerte, since you are so slim,
Since God made you the switch to scourge my flesh,
Because such pining animates your thin limbs,
Like reedy poplars swaying to April's breath.
—*Richard Dehmel*

Even though she was getting up there at the age of thirty-eight and harbored an insuperable aversion to men as sexual beings, you couldn't really call Aunt Gerta an old *maid*. The verse by Dehmel chosen as the epigraph for this chapter fitted her perfectly. She was slim and tall. Deep longing shone in her eyes, even though a pince-nez framed them, and it also appeared in her gait, even though she steered an intrepid course. Moreover, she was by no means a prude. On the contrary, in her presence matters might be discussed that would have made other ladies flee the room in shame.

Aunt Gerta was a so-called New Woman. A suffragette, she wrote poetry and read adventuresome books—but also the very best: one of her characteristics was a marked preference for art and literature of the grotesque and uncommon variety. She had a passion for nudes and statues of comely ladies, in particular. Her walls featured drawings by Beardsley and Behmer, as well as photographs of naked beauties. Aunt Gerta's favorite readings included Oscar Wilde, Platen, and Scheerbart—along with classics like Plato's *Apology*.

She dressed simply and tastefully. Instead of a corset, she wore white linen, a starched collar, and cuffs. You couldn't tell her vigorous handwriting apart from a man's. She also possessed a handsome collection of weapons. There was always a revolver on her nightstand.

Aunt Gerta was rich, but she didn't skimp when it came to financial outlays. Whenever she spotted a good book or a pretty picture that caught her fancy, she went ahead and bought it. Her traffic with relatives followed convention and was warmer only when it came to her nephew Ludwig, who was a little younger. He shared her interests—albeit with more of a focus on masculine culture, even though his own face was rather soft and displayed feminine qualities. He'd often come and visit Aunt Gerta and her lady companion, Fräulein Hagedorn.

Fräulein Hagedorn was Aunt Gerta's only female friend. They never parted each other's company. Small and delicate, but corpulent, she wore her curly black hair short and had a well-defined mouth and big brown eyes that bespoke cleverness. She always dressed just like Aunt Gerta—indeed, strangers often took them for sisters.

One day, a great commotion befell the city. Fräulein Hagedorn had left town for a few days, and a shot rang out from Aunt Gerta's apartment. The door was promptly broken down: there lay Aunt Gerta lifeless, smoking revolver in hand. A letter was addressed to "Gentleman-Reporters." Laconically, it declared: "Write only: unhappy in love!"

"Aha!" people said. "Nephew Ludwig!" Solicitous neighbors had long known that their relationship was something special.

Nephew Ludwig didn't even show up for the reading of the will. "Well," people said, "When you're so sure about things . . ."

The will declared Fräulein Hagedorn the sole heir to Aunt Gerta's estate. When she heard, she sank into her leather armchair, sobbing. "Dear, dear Gert!" she cried. Everyone was quite surprised.

But when Nephew Ludwig was told about Aunt Gerta's final decision, it proved just as astonishing. He remained quite calm and declared: "'In the beginning was Sex, and without it was not any thing made that was made,' *dixit* Przybyszewski." People shook their heads. They thought the opposite had been true in Aunt Gerta's case. Still, they deemed it natural enough that a nephew disinherited by a Rich Aunt should suffer from some kind of mental disorder.

AUNT HENRIETTE

It goes without saying that twenty-five Rich Aunts would include a painter. The artist in question is Aunt Henriette. All she did was paint and sleep. Often enough, she did both at once. Not only did she paint landscapes, male nudes, flowers, and portraits; she also painted herself. There's no other way to explain her singular complexion. Her countenance, whereupon she artfully touched up whatever wrinkles had made bold to intrude, projected a veritable rainbow. Violet was especially pronounced. Her dress was violet, too. She said it was her favorite color. I never saw evidence to disprove this claim.

As mentioned, whenever she didn't happen to be painting, Aunt Henriette busied herself with sleeping. Whether walking, sitting, standing, or lying down—she was always asleep. And any impartial observer would have agreed her artworks had been made in a somnambulistic state.

Once I watched as she fell asleep at the easel. The brush remained pressed to the canvas. She sat there, rocking back and forth like a little flower blowing in the wind; the brush moved, too, bringing forth broad, purple strokes in horizontal arcs. Needless to say, she painted in her beloved color. When she woke up, the picture was complete. Aunt Henriette explained that the violet stripes represented cosmic peregrinations. Once upon a time, she had read Scheerbart's *The Great Race*, in which ten thousand discontented worm-spirits undertake curious wanderings through the cosmos. Aunt Henriette pictured such journeys in a lilac light. She couldn't understand the author, of course: Scheerbart doesn't write for old aunts.

But Aunt Henriette acted as if he did, and she was always quoting him. So she painted backgrounds for the cosmic wanderings—which were purple, too. After all, she thought, her paintings should look proper, and she completely agreed with Scheerbart: "Yes, yes—there must be a foil for propriety—otherwise, it just turns into something common!" Well, everyone knows: when lady-painters start interpreting, something terrifying happens.

In a word: I lost my inheritance from Aunt Henriette. She saw red and grew blue in the face when she heard my verses:

> My dear Aunt Henriette!
> Sleep abed when the sun has set,
> And sleep at the easel by day,
> Paint violet lands, skies, and seas
> From Greenland to the West Indes,
> Just leave Scheerbart away!
> Not for aunts are worlds that whirl

In worlds out in space, old girl—
The cosmos is vast. Go ahead, paint
What you will a thousand times
And as many astral, ultraviolet lines:
It's still all a female complaint.

The purple poem precipitated the repeal of previous provisions for my person: Aunt Henriette disowned me. I rushed to befriend Paul Scheerbart. Since my good aunt was always off on his Great Race in her dreams, I thought he'd be named in my stead. How wrong I was! Aunt Henriette bequeathed everything to somebody named Bürger. It was a case of mistaken identity. In one of her somnambulistic trances, she'd had a vision, and so a train conductor from Rixdorf became her sole heir. For Aunt Henriette, everything was bathed in a higher light.

AUNT JULIE

———

Aunt Julie held me quite close to her heart. The sole relative to believe in my literary talents, she was also the only one whose sense of pride didn't suffer from having a poet-nephew.

When I was in the fourth grade, she already showed me kindly attention, listened to my poems ridiculing teachers, and now and then gave me change I'd use to buy chocolate, and later cigarettes. On my fifteenth birthday, she let me get my first shave. When I'd grown, she mortally offended me with the token of a nickel. I started to hit her up for bigger and bigger sums—with the result, most often, of her informing me, to her regret, that the money was invested somewhere and she didn't have even a mark left to give me. But twice she gave me one mark fifty, with great ceremony. That made a lasting impression.

Once, when I had assaulted her with some dozen new poems and she was just sitting there in stupefaction, I proposed that she fund the publication of my works. Winking at me sidelong, she said, "When I'm no longer around, my boy. Then you'll inherit 100,000 marks and you can have your poems published."

Naturally, I was ecstatic—especially when she committed her intentions to writing in my presence.

I now had a Rich Aunt. In her honor, I amassed a mountain of debts and intoned rapturous hymns.

Aunt Julie's death was a long time coming. At long last, the weakness of age set in. When she felt that the end was approaching, she had me summoned to her bedside.

She was already very weak as she took my head into her thin hands. Her lips were moving, as if she had something important to tell me. When she couldn't bring forth what was in her heart, with a faint smile she gestured to the washstand and stammered, "drawer." Then her eyes closed and she breathed her last.

I dashed to the washstand and opened it, hoping to find a check for the 100,000 marks bequeathed to me. But instead there lay a letter, written in an unsteady hand. It went as follows:

My Dear Nephew!
I thank you from the bottom of my heart for all the pleasure your art has given me. Unfortunately, my bequest will not be enough to publish your poems. I'm sure you will achieve prominence on your own. All I have is in the safe: 70 marks. Take it and pay for my burial. But keep my note, where I willed 100,000 marks to you, in

enduring memory of an aunt who had no money but a good heart and the best of intentions to see you prosper.

Hugs and kisses,
Your aunt,
Julie

Aunt Julie is to be credited with many of the doubts I harbor about Rich Aunts.

AUNT KUNIGUNDE

———

The following conversation occurred between Eugen Schmälzel, *studiosus juris*, and his aunt Kunigunde:

Aunt Kunigunde: It can't go on like this, dear Eugen. This time, I'll pay the fine, because, after all, you are my little brother's son. But it's the last time. Remember that!

Eugen: But auntie, where's your sense of humor? Come on, the prank was great; admit it was worth five marks—breaking the streetlight just when that girl was standing there reading a letter from her sweetheart?

Aunt Kunigunde: No, to be perfectly honest, it wasn't funny at all. Who knows how long she'd been waiting for that letter—and just when she gets it, you go and spoil her whole mood.

Eugen: Pff, mood! How can you be such a boor! Moods are for people who don't have a sense of humor. You, of all people, should have one.

Aunt Kunigunde: And why's that?

Eugen: Well, I mean, 'cause of your funny name.

Aunt Kunigunde: Eugen, I won't allow—

Eugen: Well, there you go. You just don't like fun!

Aunt Kunigunde (after some reflection): You're right, my dear nephew. My name is Kunigunde, and I will honor it. Once I've died, you'll see that my will is the best joke any aunt has ever made.

Eugen: Oh yes, auntie. It's much better to come into an inheritance when it's fun, too. When I raise the first glass to your eternal reward, it'll be like you're saying, "Cheers!"

Aunt Kunigunde: Go on now, my boy! I need a little time to arrange my testament.

Eugen (embracing her): Auntie! You're a treasure! The good Lord really had a twinkle in his eye when he made you. (*Exit.*)

Aunt Kunigunde: Just you wait . . .

A few months later, Aunt Kunigunde went home to the good Lord. Posthaste, Nephew Eugen headed to court for the opening of the will. He thought his funny aunt would have the inheritance of 100,000 marks paid out in change. Or maybe she'd written the document in iambic pentameter.

But Aunt Kunigunde had a wicked sense of humor. Eugen Schmälzel was disinherited. That's funny, isn't it? It didn't destroy his mood, because people with a sense of humor don't suffer from moods. All the money was set aside to start a satirical journal: *Aunt Kunigunde*. Eugen was offered the editorship, with an annual salary of 1,200 marks.

But Eugen didn't take the position. For some reason, he couldn't think of anything funny to say.

AUNT LUDOVIKA

————

Some people feel that anything painful is embrarrassing. I'm one of them. There are also people who find everything that pains them somehow pleasant. Aunt Ludovika belonged to their ranks. She was an interesting case for the psychologists—what they call a *masochist*.

If I were speaking to children, I'd explain masochism like this: a masochist is somebody who's a good little boy or girl but gets a whipping anyhow. Since I'm talking to adults, I'll say: a masochist is somebody who reads Dolorosa—and the poems this lady writes are *masochistic*, because "love and affection" rhymes with "physical correction."

So Aunt Ludovika was a masochist. She read Dolorosa, practiced Catholicism, mortified her flesh, and longed for the day when a man would come to administer these rigors lovingly.

Aunt Ludovika also had a nephew. This is commonly the case with aunts: they have one or several nephews, insofar as the latter are not, in the fact, nieces. The nephew in question was named Otto.

But Otto wasn't very educated. He hadn't read Dr. Veriphantor's study of flagellantism, Krafft-Ebing's *Psychopathia Sexualis*, or my own title on homosexuality. As such, he viewed Ludovika's fondness for Dolorosetta's poems as an aesthetic misstep, and he made a point of giving her presents of verse he deemed more suitable— especially books by Margarete Beutler, which, in a sign of loyal friendship, I'd permitted to be dedicated to me. (I confess: the volume at hand almost included "Aunt Lene" from her pen; it was already available when I started, but because of distraction on my part, or maybe something else, things didn't work out.)

One evening, Otto betook himself to Aunt Ludovika's to see whether the hideous stuff she liked reading wouldn't soon lead to her demise. Witnessing the death of a Rich Aunt is an uplifting sight, even for a person as good as Nephew Otto. After all, he told himself, he was hardly acting in his own interest by recommending better poetry to his aunt. That's just how he was: he was a very good person.

And so, one evening, he paid Aunt Ludovika a visit. As he stood outside and knocked on the door, he heard whimpering. Aghast with hope, he rushed inside. A dreadful scene awaited him. Stark naked, her withered breasts covered only by thin strands of gray hair hanging over her ears, the lamentable old lady lay on her chaise longue. Before her stood an old man in rolled-up shirt-sleeves who was trying, with quaking hands, to lash Aunt

Ludovika's back with a whip. It was an exercise in frustration: his spindly members could barely lift the heavy instrument, and his every heave landed on the back of the chair. All the same, Aunt Ludovika was whimpering piteously.

Otto was, as mentioned, quite uneducated. He didn't know that the old gentleman was simply trying to display sadistic love by torturing his estimable aunt—who, for the first time in her venerable life, had found a paramour in the want ads. A *sadist* is someone who administers punishment to a *masochist* (cf. previous entry).

Naturally, being the good person and loving nephew that he was, Otto took action. Availing himself of his pocketknife, he ran it through the elderly gentleman's chest with a cry of victory. The senior citizen spiraled to the ground; cascading jets of his heart's blood anointed the bare, yellow back of his victim as he wheezed, "Ludovika, I love you!" Then he expired.

It goes without saying that as Aunt Ludovika's naked limbs embraced the mortal remains of her beloved, his blood mixed with her tears—and that Otto bore the gore-soaked pocketknife aloft, his savior's countenance beaming in triumph. Likewise, it goes without saying that once her dolent ejaculations were spent and she had heaped execration upon the assassin of her golden years' happiness, Ludovika called the police. As a matter of course, the dead old man was trundled off to the morgue, Otto to jail, and Aunt Ludovika to the madhouse.

Finally, it goes without saying that the daughter of the murdered man—in younger years, before becoming a sadist, he had sired a love child—sued for damages. Aunt Ludovika's assets devolved to her: supplied with a dowry, the girl could stop walking the streets and enjoy the status of a lawfully wedded wife.

Incidentally, Aunt Ludovika soon died in the asylum from the effects of her alienation. The suit for damages filed by her lover's daughter made explicit disinheritance of Nephew Otto a moot point. If Otto had, in fact, gotten anything from her, the story would have proven utterly worthless for the purposes of the book at hand. So there's a bright side to the sad course of events, after all.

AUNT MIRIAM

———

I'm sincerely grateful to the siblings Florian and Adele Listig: they thwarted Aunt Miriam's efforts to make their kith and kin, Cousin Max, sole heir to her fortune. If they hadn't, my whole doctrine would be disproven.

Max was a good boy, and he sincerely loved his aunt. Unfortunately, he didn't inhabit the same town, but at the distance of a day's travel. Had he lived in the same city, indeed on the same street—as Florian and Adele did—he wouldn't have forfeited the inheritance, at least a third of which he'd been counting on.

You couldn't say that Florian and Adele loved their Aunt Miriam. All the same, they visited her often, asked about her health, and did everything else that legacy-hunting nephews and nieces are wont to do for a wealthy relative's money. But Aunt Miriam observed them with a watchful eye—she'd accidentally poked out the other knitting—and could tell the difference between her brother's children, Florian and Adele, and her sister's son, Max.

Accordingly, she made provisions in her last will and testament for Max to be the sole heir as long as, by the time she was buried, he, a good Catholic, had converted to her—Mosaic—faith.

She died suddenly, in immediate consequence of the terror Florian and Adele inspired when they marched into her room with murderous intent, chanting "Hep hep"—the refrain of an old song attending pogroms in the erstwhile German Confederation.

Even before a coffin had been built for Aunt Miriam's mortal remains, her wicked niece and nephew headed to court and greedily had her will opened. Well, they got what was coming to them. Hee hee!

Of course, if they weren't going to get anything, then Aunt Miriam's favorite, Nephew Max, shouldn't get anything, either. But how could they cheat him out of it?

There was no way to keep their aunt's death a secret. Somebody else would tell him. It was also impossible not to mention the provisions she'd made: they knew Aunt Miriam had often said, in Max's presence, that she would stipulate conditions for her burial. No way he wouldn't ask. Then Florian struck on a clever plan. He wrote his cousin a letter of condolence and felicitation sharing Aunt Miriam's dispensation—with the slight modification that his conversion to Judaism not occur prior to the funeral, but on the same day. The day in question, he indicated, was Saturday, at eight in the morning.

The letter reached Max Thursday evening. "Aha!" he thought, "You presume it can't be done before tomorrow at eight. But where does it say it has to be before the funeral? 'On the same day' means 'before sunset'!" So Max bought two black ribbons, tied one around his top hat and the other around his left arm, and set out for the service.

The interment took place right on time. It was solemn, indeed.

"Well," Florian asked his cousin after the burial. "Is everything in order?"

"Not yet," Max replied with a gloomy air of ceremony. "I'm going to see the rabbi." If he expected any protest from Florian and Adele, he was quite mistaken.

Graciously, they conceded that the day of burial did, in fact, last all day. They told him to enjoy his circumcision.

"I was wrong about them," mumbled Max as he hastened to the nearest synagogue.

"You vont vhat?" squawked Rabbi Israel Hersch when Max had presented the item of business, "I should tsirkumtsise you on shabbos? Are you meshugga? Not right in ze head? Sooner I give you all my *tsores* zhan tsircumtsise you on shabbos. *Tsu gezunt!* Come back vhen is not yontef!"

Florian and Adele Listig sat at the window smirking as Max trudged by, crestfallen. He took action against his uncle's children for willful misrepresentation, and legal expenses swallowed up a whole lot of money. Even though they received a reprimand, they had nothing to give him. And Aunt Miriam's stipulation hadn't been fulfilled.

Max duly renounced the faith of his aunt-cestors and became an anti-Semitic deputy in the Reichstag.

AUNT NANNY

———

I never found an aunt more unlikeable than Aunt Nanny. Starting with her appearance: she was like a beanpole with sparse, gray hair, a proboscis that seemed prehensile, and a voice that squeaked and snorted like a steam whistle.

Being in her presence was unbearable. She had a new maid every week, and I was the sole relation who ever came calling. I observed the practice only in consideration of the fact that, inasmuch as old ladies tend not to live forever, her whole fortune would necessarily fall to me if I didn't neglect her.

Aunt Nanny's favorite activity was delivering moral lectures. Her edifying sermons rained abuse, in language that can't be printed here, on every last person about whom she had ever heard, read, dreamed, or thought anything incompatible with the core principles of archauntiness. As for herself, Aunt Nanny could be nothing but supremely content. She expressed pride in the moral conduct of her life, interjecting mention of her "quiet reserve" at every opportunity and extolling her filthy avarice as "prudent moderation."

Nobody knew anything precise about Aunt Nanny's past. It wasn't even clear whether, by means of her beastliness or in spite of her exemplary bearing, she had ever managed to win a husband's affections—or, alternatively, whether some poor bastard had taken the desperate step of committing suicide by marrying her and allowing himself to be driven to the grave in disgust. No one was permitted to say "Missus" or "Miss"—just "Ma'am," which left room for a host of interpretations.

Luckily enough, it didn't take long for Aunt Nanny to die. Beneath her bedroom window stood a bench in the shade of an ancient and majestic linden tree. Here, one gentle evening in spring, a youth declared his love to a young maid. The kisses and caresses of the happy, budding specimens of human nature disturbed Aunt Nanny's rest. She threw the window open and, in a rage, emptied that vessel of modesty even old aunts require onto the heads of the unsuspecting lovebirds. Alas, moral indignation, perhaps jealousy, and, to be sure, the cold night air prompted her to fall ill. Within a few days, as I faithfully ministered to her on her sickbed, Aunt Nanny passed from this world.

I arranged for her to be buried as quickly as possible—the sight of her corpse was almost more revolting than her appearance in life—and set about looking for the will. She hadn't left one. Since no other close relation was around, I submitted my claim to her estate to the courts.

But what happened? One day, an elderly gentleman knocked at my door and introduced himself as the husband of the departed, Aunt Nanny of blessed memory. Twenty-seven years ago, after approximately fourteen days of wedlock, he'd wisely made himself scarce. Since the gentleman could prove that Aunt Nanny really had been his bride and that he'd had the foresight not to seek a divorce, he cheerfully raked in the whole inheritance, then shook my hand in condolence.

The time I'd spent in Aunt Nanny's company, in sickness and in health, was lost forever.

AUNT OLLY

Viktor Eberhard Dachreiter was declared sole heir in Aunt Olly's will and acceded to all rights of the same when he took into his possession the sizeable fortune of the late Olga Weidenbaum, deceased 27 October 19. . . .

When I heard, I was crushed. Upon receiving word that Aunt Olly had hanged herself, I felt the foundations of my Doctrine of Rich Aunts—which was and is meant to assure my renown for the ages—shaking underfoot. Still, I hoped that a miracle would avert further disaster. In vain! Viktor Eberhard Dachreiter had become Aunt Olly's heir.

Was I now to believe that my edifice no longer stood on solid ground? Might I yet find consolation in the elegant but trite dictum that there's an exception to every rule? I couldn't. I thought and thought. I pondered and brooded. There had to be a hitch.

I found it: the very same hook where Aunt Olly had hitched the rope, setting an end to her days for reasons unknown.

When reasons unknown are no longer unknown—I said to myself—then they are known; perforce, known reasons provide a firmer foundation than unknown grounds. I had to save my Doctrine of Rich Aunts. I would spare no effort; the end justified the means. I had to get to the bottom of it all, the real dirt.

Availing myself of a skeleton key, I entered Aunt Olly's erstwhile lodgings by night and rifled through everything that bore witness to her earthly sojourn.

Material riches were not my concern. This breaking and entry was a matter of ideals. Accordingly, I pocketed the hundred-mark bill I happened to find only because it might prove useful in the course of further research. Praise the Lord! I managed to keep it in reward for effort spent. Among her papers, I also struck upon the following.

1. A newspaper announcement declaring "The engagement of Miss Marianne Liebenstern and Captain Konrad Leo Dachreiter, ret."
2. A birth certificate dated 7 May 18. . . , registering the delivery of a male infant by Olga Weidenbaum, unwed.
3. A document attesting that (a) First Lieutenant Konrad Leo Dachreiter acknowledges the paternity of Viktor Eberhard, born 7 May 18. . . to Olga Weidenbaum, unwed; and (b) that said child is authorized to use his father's surname in public life.

4. Assorted letters from First Lieutenant, then Captain (ret.) Konrad Leo Dachreiter to "Dear Olly" promising marriage.
5. Assorted letters from my enviable friend, Viktor Eberhard Dachreiter, to Miss Olga Weidenbaum with the heading, "Dear Aunt Mama!"

Aha! I thought as I compared items one and four, glancing sidelong to where Aunt Olly had finally gotten hitched.

My theory was safe and sound.

AUNT PAULA

The main character of this chapter isn't Aunt Paula herself. It's her poodle Blackie.

For Aunt Paula had a poodle, as many ladies who are getting on in years, whom fate has denied a husband, will seek consolation in one sweet creature or another.

Besides Blackie the poodle, there was a human being to whom Aunt Paula devoted her affection. That was her nephew Eduard. Indeed, she owed the dignified station of aunt to his existence. And he, for his part, clung to the fallacious belief that Aunt Paula was *his* Rich Aunt.

Needless to say, Blackie and Eduard didn't get along. After all, this is a story about a Rich Aunt, a poodle, and a nephew.

To be sure, in Aunt Paula's presence, Blackie would wag his tail sanctimoniously; Eduard always produced a lump of sugar and lovingly offered it to the charming little beast. But whenever the two met in Aunt Paula's absence, the whole house would echo with the mutt's malicious barking—and the bone-chilling howls that followed upon the kicks Eduard administered to the creature's snout.

When the three of them went for a stroll, Aunt Paula—whose remarkable thinness was matched by her prodigious height—would walk in the middle. To her left strode Eduard, and to her right trotted Blackie. Through Aunt Paula's legs, each of her attendants would gaze upon the other in mortal enmity.

Their hatred stemmed from mutual jealousy. Blackie was jealous of Eduard because he felt deprived of every morsel of sugar the latter put in his coffee; any affectionate glance his mistress sent Eduard's way really belonged to him, Blackie thought. Eduard had more foresight. He knew that he was Aunt Paula's only blood relation, but he recognized that her love for the poodle exceeded her love for his own person; as soon as her eyes had closed forever, the dog wouldn't have a single care in the world. Indeed, Eduard was afraid lest the provisions made for Blackie's comfort and care surpass what little was left for him.

Eduard reckoned that such a catastrophe might be avoided if the dog shuffled off this mortal coil before Aunt Paula did. But since the animal was hale and hearty—and his Aunt wrinkly and wheezy—it would be best to eliminate the danger the cur represented as soon as possible.

And so, Eduard hatched a dark scheme.

The daily walk made by Aunt Paula and her stalwart companions passed over a footbridge above a deep body of water. Here, the dreadful deed would occur . . .

It was a Sunday, before noon. In the waves of the little stream over which the aforementioned bridge led, the sun was playing hide-and-seek: creeping behind the clouds, then bursting forth to kiss all that its light bathed in overflowing tenderness. In short: a mood prevailed that I might hope to convey if, first, I possessed any talent as a lyric poet, and, second, if only I had as much time as someone enjoying a leisurely retirement. Since neither is the case, suffice it to say that in such a mood Aunt Paula, along with her two bosom friends, bestrode this setting with a dignified step beseeming the circumstances.

Eduard gushed about the wonderful weather and lovely surroundings. He drew the attention of his aunt, who was touched by his solicitude, to the green slopes running down to the water, and he pointed to where a bouquet of forget-me-nots might be easily obtained.

With a cry of delight, Aunt Paula rushed to do just that—which is precisely what her cunning heir was waiting for. Until this point, the poodle had been jogging along indifferently, daintily passing the time snapping at flies. Now, behind Aunt Paula's back, Eduard gave the poodle a kick in the flank. Squealing in pain, Blackie plummeted into the deep.

Aunt Paula's horror was so great she almost did the same. But she managed not to and instead threw herself at faithless Eduard's feet. Sobbing, she implored him to save the poor beast now howling and paddling around, trying in vain to clamber up the steep embankment.

Eduard intoned a long-winded lecture as his aunt begged his mercy, endeavoring to demonstrate that the dog's salvation would occur only at great risk to his own life. Aunt Paula heard only Blackie's miserable howls and entreated him, with greater and greater insistence, not to let her little dear drown. To no avail.

So she changed her tune and issued a command—which didn't help, either. Finally, overcome by rage, she barked: "I'm disinheriting you, you heartless monster!" That did the trick.

Calling to mind Schiller's poem, "The Diver," Eduard boldly plunged into the drink. With vigorous strokes, he neared the dog. But when he had just grabbed the collar—not to pull the creature under the water altogether, but just to immerse its muzzle for long enough to get the air out—Blackie's teeth bit Eduard's hand, down to the bone. In a spirited leap, the poodle jumped up to Aunt Paula—who, overcome by joy at having her little treasure back, failed to remark that her exsanguinated nephew Eduard was in the course of drowning.

They fished his body out and brought it to the house. Deeply moved, she arranged for a gravestone with the inscription:

To the brave savior of my dear doggy, the man who gave his life in love to me and my poodle.
    In gratitude, Aunt Paula.

Blackie inherited everything. And when Blackie died, the remainder of Aunt Paula's fortune went to found the "Eduard Schwarz Trust for Shipwrecked Mariners."

AUNT Q

I butchered my weak old aunt,
She was already unwell and shaking,
I rummaged around at her haunt,
To find anything at all worth taking.

Frank Wedekind will forgive me if I beat him to the punch and shine some light on the butchered aunt. She belongs in our Aunthology since her case demonstrates some of the miscalculations that one may make. That said, to avoid being indiscreet, I'll call the protagonist of the story Aunt Q: on othe one hand, because it fits the alphabet, but also because Q is the only letter for which the good Lord did not create a woman's name; as such, no one will feel directly implicated.

Aunt Q was a lady who, for forty-five years, lodged on the third floor of a building in northwest Berlin and occupied two rooms (including the kitchen).

Aunt Q would rise at six o'clock, mix some chicory and hot water to brew what she called "coffee," and set about domestic tasks. The latter involved determining whether all the doors were locked, checking to see if savings kept in the third drawer of an iron safe had remained untouched, sweeping all the nooks and crannies lest one of them harbor a copper penny (thirty-seven years ago, it seems, Aunt Q had struck upon one under the kitchen table!), and beating the dust out of all the clothing and furniture—because you never know . . .

She performed these chores in a negligée, that is, a nightshirt and petticoat. On top, she wore a blue apron that doubled as a handkerchief.

Aunt Q would attire herself properly around eleven. This meant throwing a black wool frock over her petticoat and, over her nightshirt (and the humpback underneath) a red Turkish shawl, which she tucked in the front. She then covered her patchy, greenish hair with a peaked straw hat, whose long ribbons fastened under her wobbly chin. Finally, she took in hand a mighty blue umbrella with a massive wooden handle and grabbed her key ring.

Then she went to do her shopping. As she left the building, she never failed to impress on the concierge that, for heaven's sake, no one be admitted to her apartment—a sheer impossibility given that not just the door to her dwelling, but also the doors within, all the closets, and every last drawer had been equipped with a complicated locking mechanism she carefully activated whenever she left.

Well, Aunt Q had a nephew. As a token of my esteem for Frank Wedekind, I will leave the party unnamed.

This nephew was a miserable creature and Aunt Q's sole relation.

Since Aunt Q never displayed any signs of illness and also neglected to make the slightest provisions in the event of her demise, said nephew could not but feel the weight of destiny bearing upon him. He bought a knife and used it to slaughter the old woman after spending the night at her dwelling.

He did so as follows. One day, he happened upon Aunt Q as she was out and about at the market and offered his manly protection. Since Aunt Q suspected nothing malicious on the part of her own kin, she was genuinely moved and requested further assistance. He escorted her home and then, with the affectionate loyalty beseeming a nephew, offered to be her buckler until the following day. Aunt Q fell for it.

Need I describe how the murderer massacred his victim? I fear lest harm befall lady readers with a delicate nervous constitution. Let me simply mention Frank Wedekind's apposite poem, which may be consulted in his *Princess Russalka* or Bierbaum's anthology, *Brettl-Lieder*.

The key point, to my mind, is that the murderous nephew found nothing in the assorted coffers and chests other than rags and a check for a thousand marks. (On this score, Wedekind has indulged in a bit of poetic license.) Efforts to cash the check produced two immediate effects: first, it was determined that the expiry date had long passed, and second, the necessitous youth was taken into custody.

The state pocketed Aunt Q's money. The murderer was executed at Plötzensee Prison.

And that's the gruesome tale of Aunt Q—so gruesome, in fact, that I'm eager to drop the whole thing and move on to Aunt Rosa, whose story is also quite interesting.

AUNT ROSA

———

Let me confess: I'm not crazy about discussing Aunt Rosa. I'm a bit of a moralist, and the old lady is such a villainous character I'd prefer not to have anything to do with her—especially since she's still alive and there's no telling how she might exact revenge.

Whenever a young man or a young lady has a rich aunt, a little inheritance-coveting is only natural—even though, as this book makes plain, it's really no use. Aunt Rosa is such a base creature that she covets her own money. And not a little.

When Aunt Rosa was somewhere in her sixties, her niece Thekla, who'd just gotten married to a traveling wine salesman, took her in. Supposedly, she extended this welcome so the old lady, who was quite alone in the world, would be well taken care of. In fact, the idea was that—during the hours, days, and weeks her gentleman-husband was attending to professional duties—her self-sacrificing and solicitous attentions might induce the old dear to write a will that would make feeding her a joy to the end.

At first, the crafty aunt proved obliging. The will was written. When the wine merchant returned from one of his trips, Thekla, who always pined for him to the point of taking ill on the seventh day—and sometimes in the course of the week, too—rushed to embrace her spouse. She cried for a while and then, because it was already eight o'clock, rustled him into the bedroom. Around midnight, after formal greetings had been completed, she started elaborating plans for the future on the basis of the will, which declared the couple sole heirs to Aunt Rosa's three million. It was resolved to pamper the good woman to death and lay her to rest—and then make up for the love and affection lengthy commercial engagements had made them miss.

A new life would begin. Having observed due diligence, the two lovebirds fell asleep in the early hours; they didn't rise until noon, when they emerged in a somewhat pale and depleted state.

The plans systematized that memorable night began in earnest. Soon, Thekla showed signs that gladsome tidings lay in store. Now the blissfully happy couple knew that their purposes also served an Eternal Design.

Aunt Rosa grew thinner and thinner. Three quarters of a year later, when little Bruno was lifted from the baptismal font—that is, when godmotherly duties had been fulfilled—people had no doubt that the kingdom of heaven was at hand.

But even though she dried up like the stalk of a buttercup, Aunt Rosa had no intention of dying. Year after year passed. The traveling salesman grew old and gray. Thekla's charms withered. Still, her husband set out with his wines and spirits, and when duty kept him from the roost on Saturdays, his wife suffered as much as before.

Little Bruno battened. At a tender age, he already understood his role and brought his parents boundless joy by vexing and grieving the old lady—who only grew thinner, yellower, and even more decrepit. On the rare occasion that a somewhat fatter portion fell to her, Bruno would rush in and gobble it up before her eyes.

The parents acquired a parrot to secure their son's position. Lore, the bird, and Bruno, the boy, split the work: the former would squawk and, as soon as the aunt turned her head, the latter would take possession of her dish; conversely, Bruno would hoot, and as soon as Aunt Rosa looked over, Lore would flap in and seize the biggest morsel on her plate.

Before long, Aunt Rosa had grown so emaciated she couldn't even walk. So she sat in a leather armchair, dripping from the eyes, nose, and mouth, redolent of the sweat of her brow and armpits.

Well, the man and wife who had taken the old lady into their care hardly lacked refinement. Indeed, Thekla was wont to compose verses on those Saturdays that business kept her spouse away. One of her especially ardent poems even appeared in *Gesellschaft*. So it's no wonder that the spectacle Aunt Rosa presented—the noises issuing from her nose and lower abdomen, the fragrance oozing from her every pore—only fired the couple's desire to lay hold of her three million once and for all.

So they let her go hungry and "wear the Lenten veil." She almost ate it, too. But fasting suited her: the thinner she grew, the less of a body there was to mortify. And she was as strong of spirit as she'd ever been (even though that's not saying much).

Thekla and her husband are long dead. Bruno is now an elderly bachelor. Aunt Rosa's tenacity made him so grumpy that no girl would have him. When he goes, their line will be extinct.

But Aunt Rosa has no intention of dying. She's so stingy she doesn't want anyone to get her money. She intends to live until social progress has overcome capitalism. Then her fortune won't be worth a thing.

Aunt Rosa sits in the chair, gnawing at her veil, oozing, grunting, and stinking. But that's just her. *Pecunia non olet.*

AUNT SOPHIE

———

Dr. Friedrich Süsslieb rang the bell again—for the third time now, and quite vigorously. Finally, he heard shuffling within, then steps dragging toward the door.

After turning the key twice and pushing back the deadbolt, Aunt Sophie opened up.

"Well, well, well, Fritsch," her toothless maw hissed, "Look who'ss dessided to drop in!"

Friedrich presented a bouquet to her and showed his best manners, even though the smell in the room—which Aunt Sophie carefully sealed off with another turn of the key—invited a different kind of response. Nothing here was especially cozy. The sofa and chairs were shrouded in musty, gray cloth, as if the occupant had set off on an extended voyage. Dense cobwebs clung to the pictures and corners in the apartment. Contemplating Aunt Sophie herself, the nattily attired Dr. Süsslieb couldn't suppress a shudder.

A viscous bead was hanging from her long, crooked nose. It never left: whenever it reached her mouth and a spotted tongue had wiped it away, another took its place. Aunt Sophie's gibbous, wasted frame was arrayed in a dirty brown dress, torn and stitched back together at various locations. The sharp, black nails of her withered, bony hand scratched constantly at a reddish bald spot on her head.

Fortunately, Aunt Sophie was hard of hearing. Accordingly, her devoted nephew—between assorted snatches of verbiage about how things were going, the lovely weather, heartfelt greetings from his wife, and so on—managed to mutter less friendly words under his breath: "damned old witch, hideous tightwad, if only you'd hurry up and croak," and sundry other terms of endearment.

In the corner of the room stood a dusty safe; both aunt and nephew intermittently cast sidelong glances in its direction. That was the bond that united them: all her loving care, and his every hope, focused on that old piece of furniture . . .

Aunt Sophie received visitors frequently. In addition to Dr. Friedrich Süsslieb, three nephews and four nieces would check in to see how she was doing, gaze longingly at the safe, and wish their aunt good health and a long life when they departed.

She died at last. The nephews and nieces all came for the opening of the will. Aunt Sophie's final wishes read:

> I don't want my smirking heirs to be happy about my death. I bequeath my fortune to St. John's Parish.

When the family members approached Aunt Sophie's casket, they saw a spiteful grin on her wrinkly face . . .

I'm aware that the tale of Aunt Sophie is rather crude. But there's no helping it, and at least the story shouldn't be difficult to believe. I hope critics won't find fault with me: Aunt Sophie's the one lacking sophistication. The next case will more than make up for that.

AUNT THERESE

———

The story of Aunt Therese's life, to the extent it concerns us here—that is, the beginning of the end—starts with the death of her nephew Willy. Willy is now thirty-two. I first met him when Aunt Therese had been lying in the grave for a week.

At a young age, the orphaned son of Aunt Therese's departed sister—and the only prospective heir to the goodly aunt's inheritance—had set out into the big, wide world: the wilds of the American West. Because he'd been given a proper upbringing, he sent his inconsolable aunt a postcard every fourteen days. When he really needed money, he even sent letters.

But Aunt Therese was convinced: young people mustn't be spoiled. If you support them and indulge their every whim—after all, what does a young man want money for?—then licentiousness and excess are the result. And a close relative and pious Christian should never encourage that. Such reasoning buttressed her natural inclination to save money for Nephew Willy so he would preserve her in blessed memory for that much longer when he finally inherited it.

Accordingly, Aunt Therese experienced an especial joy when postcards arrived. She had a good heart; it pained her to no end to think that any letter from Willy would lead to his own disappointment. Whenever she received a letter, Aunt Theresa shed a tear on an international money order. Over time, the check came to consist of a single, discolored blotch. It never occurred to her that helpful resolutions, at least for some people, do occasionally prompt action.

Meanwhile, in America, Willy raged against Aunt Therese. He'd taken up with a cute little Indian girl, into whose uncorrupted, yellow-brown heart he planted a lifelong hatred for anything bearing the title of "aunt." The more he received nothing, the more he wrote nothing. Gradually, his correspondence with Aunt Therese lapsed.

Year after year went by. Willy abandoned the Wild West for the wilds of eastern Africa—although Aunt Therese wasn't apprised of the development. When she felt the end drawing near, she wrote a hearfelt missive, asking him to get in touch again. The little Indian didn't forward the letter. In the first place, she didn't know Willy's address in the wilds of eastern Africa. Second, he'd just up and left her; now, he was surely having fun with some cute little negress. So the letter was returned to sender.

Thus, Aunt Therese drenched the money order in tears and wrote a will, leaving the fortune to missionary expeditions for converting heathen aboriginal peoples. Then she went to court and declared her nephew Willy a missing person. Legally, this meant that at pain of being declared dead, he had to register his whereabouts. He failed to do so because he was busy. The little negress had given him lovely little mulatto twins, and the compounded joys of fatherhood left him no time to read the *Bulletin of the Prussian and German Empire*. After a year, the legal threat of non-existence became reality. Henceforth, Willy was officially dead.

With great effort, Aunt Therese had managed to hold out until this point. Now, unable to survive her nephew's unfortunate demise, she passed away.

Shortly beforehand, Willy had experienced a strange presentiment and set out for Europe again. He arrived just in time to behold Aunt Therese freshly dead—and rushed to court to claim his inheritance. Here, it was demonstrated to him that he had died a few days earlier; as per the law, a deceased individual, however alive said party may be, could not claim Aunt Therese's money.

A friend who knew I was researching Rich Aunts sent Willy my way.

The poor man showed up at my door. Of course, I could provide little grounds for hope. However, since I was afraid further attempts might prove availing—and, in consequence, invalidate my theory of Rich Aunts' immortality—I encouraged him to consult the materials I had gathered.

Naturally, Willy gave up on further efforts to get Aunt Therese's money. But so he wouldn't go away completely empty-handed, I promised him the twenty-fifth part—4 percent, that is—of the book's profits, corresponding to the portion devoted to his kinswoman.

Therefore, in the interest of my dear friend Willy, I urgently beseech readers to do everything in their power to ensure massive sales of my book on Rich Aunts.

What can I say? I'm a good person.

AUNT URSULA

———

When Sigismund Veilchenstock's grandfather still believed that storks brought babies, Aunt Ursula was already an heirloom the family guarded jealously. They thought she was unspeakably rich, for she hailed from Spain and displayed the most extravagant habits.

Aunt Ursula had been born in Toledo. When she ripened to a marriageable age, two grandees are said to have courted her. Indeed, rivalry prompted them to finish each other off in a duel. Such was the legend surrounding Aunt Ursula.

Her name, bearing, and appearance pointed unambiguously to the Semitic Orient. People reverently called her "the Jewess of Toledo." Later, when Sigismund Veilchenstock joined the ranks of those who attended and cherished this crown jewel of the family, her title changed. Henceforth, she was "the Eternal Jewess of Toledo."

This, in essence, is what there is to say about Aunt Ursula's persona.

Let us now take a look at the distinguished lady's person.

Aunt Ursula inhabited a garret on the fifth floor of a building at the rear of a tenement. Its domestic appointments consisted of a wobbly table and a wobbly bed. Under the mattress, it was rumored, vast treasures lay hidden.

She still wore the dress she had worn when Sigismund Veilchenstock's grandfather thought storks brought babies. Her raiment shone forth in all the colors of the rainbow: nephews and nieces of countless ages assured its preservation by supplying variegated upholstery fabrics at their own expense. The remains of a green slipper adorned her left foot, and what had been a pink one her right. The former was a tribute brought by Konrad, a nephew of the third generation, and the latter an offering made by a niece of the fourth generation, Lucia.

Aunt Ursula displayed a countenance with a yellow-gray hue, pursed together in a thousand tiny folds. Her pinched eyes still beamed cleverly, and the handful of yellow-colored hairs framing her baldness bristled affectionately whenever one of her innumerable nephews or nieces visited her chambers.

That, let it be known, happened almost every day. The callers disregarded aesthetic reservations. Surely, they thought, the treasures hidden under her mattress had a more pleasant scent than what wafted their way when entering the dwelling.

One day, Aunt Ursula fell ill. Morning and night, people ran in and out of the tiny garret. One brought wine, the other sausage, and yet another chocolate. A little niece of the sixth generation even brought her favorite doll, so that Aunt Ursula might take joy and find comfort.

Sigismund Veilchenstock was beside himself. The prospect of dividing up the old crone's loot positively transported him.

When he visited his ailing aunt, his gaze all but burned a hole through the venerable lady's decrepit frame and moldering mattress. He beheld a vision of thousands of banknotes. And when Aunt Ursula stirred and her gaunt ossature crunched, Sigismund thought he could hear the gold bullion in her couch jingling.

Aunt Ursula's worsening condition gave even more reason for joy: her forces were fading so rapidly that when the heirs offered words of comfort—telling her not to speak of dying, for it would mean their own end—the only answer she could give was a feeble grunt.

Finally, the hour was at hand. Forty-five survivors had squeezed into the little room to be present for the momentous event. More than a few feared that they would choke to death on the pestilential air before Aunt Ursula had breathed her last.

Suddenly, Aunt Ursula made a start. Every neck turned. Her legs jerked straight ahead, and her hand gestured downward, to where she had sat in times of health.

The heirs got the picture. That's where the treasure lay.

A hollow squeak, a final snort, and Aunt Ursula had passed.

Ninety greedy hands shot out to lift the body from its resting place. Following some twenty minutes of fisticuffs that produced several bloody noses, Sigismund Veilchenstock managed to lodge his dead aunt under the bed.

Well, this is the upshot: hours of searching failed to locate the fortune the heirs had anticipated for so long. In the table drawer, they found three copper pennies—and at the spot to which Aunt Ursula had pointed, the outcome of her last meal.

The heirs recouped what they could by selling Aunt Ursula's corpse to a medical school. The yield was 22.50 marks, which meant fifty cents for each heir.

Thus concludes the tale of Aunt Ursula, the Eternal Jewess of Toledo.

AUNT VERA

———

Don't think that I'm calling her Aunt Vera because I need a name with V. I could just as well have called her Aunt Violet, Aunt Veronica, or Aunt Vespasiana. But her name really was Vera. As truly as Vera means "the true one," she was the most dishonest, scheming, and two-faced creature ever to wear a petticoat.

That said, she was only dishonest, scheming, and two-faced after death. In life, Aunt Vera was a dear old white-haired and very wealthy lady to whom all her nieces and nephews showed the utmost devotion. Therein lay her stubborn mendacity.

Aunt Vera kept a very proper house. She had three rooms, a kitchen, bath, and all the appointments. She hosted guests at almost every meal. In particular, her afternoon coffees were celebrated among the young people who formed her company.

"Aunt Vera," they said, "You're the most marvelous woman on God's green earth."

Aunt Vera would laugh and be happy that they felt so at ease with her.

But one day Aunt Vera died.

The sorrow of her nephews and nieces was deep and real. The afternoon coffees were over and done. For all that, her visitors now enjoyed the prospect of a handsome inheritance. Eight of Aunt Vera's stalwarts numbered in these ranks.

Aunt Vera was laid to rest. The next day, the eight relations went to court to present their claims to her estate—Aunt Vera hadn't left a will.

Alas, cunning Destiny held an ugly strategem in store.

The judge demanded that the eight heirs prove they really were Aunt Vera's nephews and nieces.

Naturally, not a one of them had thought of this particular eventuality.

From childhood on, they'd called Aunt Vera "Aunt Vera." Never had a single one of them doubted that Aunt Vera was, in fact, an Aunt Vera.

Now they were completely flabbergasted. Aunt Vera had shamefully lied to them. She'd allowed herself to be called "Aunt" for all these years without actually being one. The heirs seethed with rage; instead of tears and gratitude, insults and curses followed Aunt Vera to the grave.

However, a very distant cousin could prove her kinship with Aunt Vera. The whole estate was hers.

The heiress didn't host afternoon coffees.

AUNT WERRA

———

You're probably wondering why Aunt Vera is followed by Aunt Werra. You think I'm just trying to show that I'm aware of an unusual variant of the same name. Please. It's not a matter of personal decision at all. Aunt Werra *is* Aunt Werra. That's right: "is"—not "was." She is named Aunt Werra. You'll see soon enough.

In fact, the story starts with Aunt Werra's late spouse, Uncle Philipp—as is only right.

At the age of thirty-two, Uncle Philipp married Aunt Werra, who was twenty-one at the time. She was a pleasant, educated, and pretty Protestant girl. He was also Protestant. Otherwise, he didn't share her qualities. At any rate, he was ugly, not pretty, and he wasn't pleasant but ill-tempered. As for his education, it was so-so. Thanks to fraud, however, he was seriously rich. He also had a hunchback, sunken belly, and runny eyes. In a word, he possessed the immense advantage of being congenitally unfit for life.

I don't want to say how long the marriage lasted, lest somebody get the idea of calculating Aunt Werra's age.

Let me simply indicate that it lasted long enough for Uncle Philipp to die at the age of forty-six. Childless, Aunt Werra was left with an immense fortune—as well as a host of impecunious nephews and nieces, a heart longing for love, and her late spouse's stipulation that, in the event of her entering into holy matrimony again, all of his money be used to build a cathedral in his own, Philippine honor.

Aunt Werra had an agreeable appearance. She dressed in pink tulle dresses with a white pinafore that complemented her thick blonde hair, full cheeks, sharp little teeth, and pert nose. Of average height, she boasted a more-than-average bosom and had the waistline of an eighty-six-year-old oak (approximately). If no one credited her late husband with having displayed undue warmth, the trait was universally remarked in her own person. Thus the rumor spread among us nephews— I don't know about the girls, since it's more fun just to touch on sensitive things with them—that Aunt Werra, in blessed selflessness, had traded the straight-and-narrow for amorous errancy. Let me stand here and put it firmly: this was shameful calumny. What subsequently occurred during Aunt Werra's widowhood proves that if suspicions had been warranted, Uncle Philipp's line wouldn't have died out with him. But I'm getting ahead of myself.

When our dear uncle was buried, Aunt Werra traded her pink dress for somber, black attire. For four months, she lived in chaste seclusion. Then she added a white lace collar to signify that she was only in half-mourning. Eventually, Aunt Werra shone forth in gay colors again, hungry for love. Indeed, she so overflowed with vitality that the oak with which I have taken the liberty of comparing her waistline assumed the dimensions of ninety-year-old timber.

To stick to the image: her trunk came to have the size of a tree that had stood for 100, 120, and then 150 years. When we, her nephews, observed that Aunt Werra was often no longer alone, but in the company of a stately gentleman, disrespectful murmurs were bruited. Even my girl cousins—her nieces—whispered all kinds of things they shouldn't have known about.

But—what else is there to say? Aunt Werra was still relatively young, and certainly young enough for love. She wasn't allowed to marry, but why should she—now that her lord and master had been pushing up daisies for over a year—not honor sentiments that are perfectly natural?

One day, Aunt Werra made a journey. Six weeks later, she returned with such a rejuvenated midriff that comparison to a seventy-four-year-old oak wouldn't be unfounded. In tow, she brought a country girl with a long, checkered hatband and a papoose in which a chubby little blonde baby was thrashing about.

The moral outrage among the nephews and nieces was unimaginable. All of them renounced our aunt. I was the only one who still paid the occasional visit. After all, the case presented matters of interest for my Aunthology.

Plus, I reasoned, even if I no longer have any hope of benefiting from Uncle Philipp's bequest in the capacity of a nephew, I shouldn't ruin my prospects for enjoying the same as a son-in-law. Aunt Werra's little bundle of joy is a girl.

As for when Aunt Werra croaks, I couldn't care less. That's just what she gets.

AUNT X

The letter x mainly plays a role in mathematics. As a rule, it represents an unknown quantity to be determined on the basis of attendent circumstances. The case of Aunt X is rather similar. I intend to tell her story to prove that, also in human life, there are mathematical existences that admit grave miscalculation if one does not solve for them correctly.

Before beginning my account of Aunt X, some information about her niece, Clärchen Meiser, is required.

She was a sweet young girl of seventeen years and a half, with luxuriant, silver-blonde tresses, dreamy eyes as blue as the sky, and a cute little button nose. Upon receipt of the vast inheritance, she planned to have a splendid empire dress made: violet, with broad half-sleeves, and a bodice embroidered in yellow silk. She thought that would be just lovely, and I also thought it would suit her delightfully. To say nothing of Karl—Karl Bohnsack! He'd turn cartwheels when he saw her in a dress like that. Karl Bohnsack was Clärchen's fiancé—they'd been engaged for a year already. As soon as the inheritance came, they'd get married. Naturally enough, she just couldn't wait.

As matters stood, things were pretty unpleasant. Karl would visit her in the evening—and then, the next morning, people would get to talking. And when she went to see him, gossip flourished in both buildings: here, it was scandalous that a girl so young had the effrontery to enter a bachelor's quarters; there, she hadn't spent the night at home *again*. Those stupid neighbors felt perfectly entitled to heap moral condemnation on young human beings just because they were fond of each other. If only what they both wanted would hurry up and come! The couple desired nothing more. Some day, Clärchen had to get all the joy she deserved.

When Clärchen was four years old, her father had died. When she was five, her mother did the same. An old aunt suddenly appeared, wearing long, pendant earrings and a black velvet dress. She set Clärchen on her lap, kissed her, and said: "One day, my child, when I'm dead, too, you'll get what's coming and inherit my whole estate." After the funeral, she vanished. The neighbors took Clärchen in and raised her—they'd heard what the old lady had told the child. But whenever they asked what her name was, all that Clärchen could tell them was "Aunt." That's what her parents had called her. Clärchen knew nothing more.

Now she was a grown-up girl, and she told herself that such an old lady couldn't possibly live forever.

Together with Karl, Clärchen piously awaited the hour when the death notice and inheritance would arrive. But nothing came. Living in anticipation for so long, the two lovers finally lost patience. They decided to find out what they could. The matter proved difficult, because Clärchen didn't have any relatives. Finally—and after considerable effort—a canny lawyer determined that Clärchen's mother had an aunt who'd emigrated to America. Her surname was Piepenmeier; he couldn't find out her first name.

Clärchen put all her stock in tracking down her mysterious relation. She set all the private eyes of North America on all the continent's Piepenmeiers. Ultimately, the measure yielded a set of twenty-four Aunt Piepenmeiers. But the one she wanted—Aunt X—wasn't included.

Then, a cataclysmic event shook Clärchen from head to toe; excitedly, she urged Karl to marry her right away. But what prospects did the couple have? He didn't have any money, and she didn't have any money yet. How was he supposed to feed a family? So they deferred the wedding until it was too late. Unmarried, Clärchen now gave suck to a miniature Karl.

Contemplating the innocent babe crying, she sat there, wondering what to do. All of a sudden, a courier appeared and handed her a cable: the American gumshoe had located Aunt X and was on the way back to Germany with her.

Clärchen's aunt arrived four weeks later. Horror of horrors! When she saw that she'd been promoted to great-great-aunt, moral outrage prompted her to disinherit her only niece and will her whole estate to a convent.

Luckily enough, joyous anticipation of the aunt's fortune and a sense of paternal pride had, in the interim, inspired a stroke of genius: Karl invented a device that soon earned so much money he could guarantee Clärchen connubial bliss and that violet empire dress with broad half-sleeves and a bodice embroidered in yellow silk.

My own investigations have determined Aunt Piepenmeier's first name. To provide a satisfying climax in this regard, too, I'd like to share it. Her name was *Xenia*.

AUNT YVETTE

As her name suggests, Aunt Yvette had been a ballerina. Indeed, the pictures hanging in her apartment—to say nothing of the tales with which she regaled visitors—convinced us that she'd been quite a beautiful one. Her erstwhile beauty also followed from the fact that she was rich. She was so rich that we were all happy to view her as our own Rich Aunt.

Funny how a beautiful ballerina can change! When I knew her, Aunt Yvette couldn't really have danced in public. Over the years, her girth had come to approach the size of a brewery carter's gut. She also resembled a deliveryman in her fondness for spirits. Whenever a caller came—and as soon as she had recovered from the asthmatic fit occasioned by salutations and hello-kisses (for profound ardor still stirred in Aunt Yvette's breast)—she immediately set some potent potation before the guest. Then she'd arrange her bracelets so the precious stones all but blinded her interlocutor, flash her false teeth at him, and proceed to carry on about this and that with great animation.

Sometimes, when the stories about other dancers started to get particularly gripping—naturally, Aunt Yvette never spoke of herself—it seemed that her glassy eyes would give an encouraging wink. Every now and then, one of the buttons securing the blouse above her expansive bosom's flabby folds flew across the room.

I was impervious to the charms of the quinquagenerian spinster, however. Fool that I was! I'm absolutely sure that if I'd been more obliging, I wouldn't be what I am today: some poor devil running up new debts while running away from old ones.

My sole consolation is that none of the other nephews took up the offer, either. My faith in the immortality of Rich Aunts stands firm.

Well, I'll just finish as best I can. One evening, I paid another visit and found her sitting cozily at the end of her plush sofa with a jovial-looking gentleman. As she teasingly ran her chubby little tadpole of a hand over his flushed face, she introduced me to an "old friend and colleague," Herr Gustav Heuforker.

"Take a good look at him," she said with a cloying grin. Mischievously, she added: "Yes indeed, my dear boy. Herr Heuforker's your uncle. We just got engaged."

Herr Gustav Heuforker has been a widower for some time now. I hear he's enjoying his freedom. And to think I have to call a man like that my uncle!

AUNT ZERLINDE

When Aunt Zerlinde passed away, so did any faith I still had that Rich Aunts are mortal beings. Since her demise, I've been sullen, skeptical, irritable, and unbelieving. She was the last pillar propping up my reverence for the title of "Rich Aunt." With its fall, the bright illusions of my youthful hopes all were buried.

Once, when I was seven years old, I naively estimated that Aunt Zerlinde was about twenty-six. Since my guess was about thirty years out of the ballpark, I became the goodly maid's favorite nephew. Aunt Zerlinde denied no request, sheltered me when I got into trouble with my parents, and even—although no relative ever believed me—gave me twenty pfennigs to buy chocolate. In a word: she spoiled me rotten.

When I was bigger, I tried to borrow some money. Aunt Zerlinde grew choked with emotion; tearfully, she told me she couldn't help me now. Thrifty and conservative, she was setting everything aside for me to inherit later on. I continued to importune her, and she showed me her will. It read:

Having failed to acknowledge my love and devotion and treat me with the respect and reverence to which I am entitled as their relation, I declare my whole circle of relatives, with the sole exception of my nephew Erich disinherited. He was a comfort to me and the church of my heart; I hereby bequeath my every mortal possession to him to do as he sees fit.

That's not a typo: there's no comma after my name, Erich. Aunt Zerlinde simply forgot to add one. In joyful anticipation of her bequest, I overlooked the omission. As the further course of events reveals, the matter proved fateful.

On the whole, I was a cautious young man. Accordingly, I beheld visions of raging fires, calamitous floods, and sundry disasters threatening the invaluable document. My vigorous appeals induced Aunt Zerlinde to promise to keep it on her person day and night. The sash at her waist, where her maidenly embonpoint was cinched, provided the hiding spot.

Weeks passed, then months. One day, Aunt Zerlinde wanted to go on a trip, and she asked me to come along. I agreed and made sure that she was bringing her will. Off we sped in the express train.

The details of the journey aren't important—they don't bear directly on the immortality of Rich Aunts. What warrants mention, however, is the fact that our train was headed straight for another one. In consequence, Aunt Zerlinde was flattened like a pancake. I managed to save myself by courageously leaping out the window, having boldly grabbed at my aunt's midriff to gain possession of her will.

Naturally enough, the virtuous spinster—to whom a man's hand had never drawn so near—cried out in chaste indignation and sought to safeguard her maidenhood. I can't blame her for the misunderstanding, and it was just my bad luck that she clung to the document the whole time. I tried to prevail upon her to let go, but the next thing I remember was lying in a heap by the tracks—and Aunt Zerlinde's corpse. All I saw after that was the snatch of paper (which had caught fire in the collision) burning to ashes in her hand.

What I managed to wrest from my unfortunate aunt that fatal hour contained only the following words:

> Having failed to acknowledge my love and devotion—
> and reverence to which I am entit—
> my nephew Erich disinherited—
> the church of my heart—
> I hereby bequeath my every mortal possession—

When my bones were halfway back in place, I set out for court with the scrap in hand. No one believed that the opening words referred to relatives she was

cutting off, and that my name indicated an exception—
otherwise, a comma would follow "Erich." To no avail!
The "Sacred Heart of Jesus Church" came along and
made off with the whole of Aunt Zerlinde's estate. That
was really stretching grammar and orthography.

I lost my own savings in countless suits against the
perfidious church, along with the boundless sympathy I
formerly reserved for Rich Aunts.

Now, I don't even believe in punctuation.

OBITUARY

So slumber gently! Peace to you at last,
Dear ones, and rest in Elysian glades!
We worried lest oblivion steal fast
And darkness swallow your shades.
Betimes, everyone seeks to grasp
At a memory when life fades—
Thus, tho' you may be rotting under the earth,
Rich Aunts, know we remember your worth.
Once we expected to be your heirs; in stealth,
We eagerly awaited your demise;
But when you died, and the prospect of wealth
Loomed before our hungry eyes,
Disappointment soon came, and we felt
Our o'erhasty hope to have been unwise.
Indeed, we faced a matter simple and true:
With Rich Aunts, it doesn't matter what you do.
This insight, though not easily paid,
Fired and fueled a new act of creation:
The book that now sees the light of day:
For your approval or disapprobation!

How you lived, died, and finally were laid
To rest, we share with the generations.
If you embody seeming, not being, which ever lies,
Grant some of your fame, which never will die!

Erik Butler has translated about a dozen academic titles, as well as literary works from French, German, Italian, and Yiddish. His own books include two studies of vampirism and a history of martial representations of language.

WAKEFIELD GALLERIES